Framed For Life

Check out the other books in the

FRIGHTVISION

series:

The Cursed Coin

Picture Day

Wishful Thinking

#GraveyardChallenge

FRIGHTVISION

Framed For Life

Artemis Hart

Bruce Zanders

Culliver Crantz

This is a work of fiction. Names, characters, places, and incidents either are the product of the author's imagination or are used fictitiously. Any resemblance to actual persons, living or dead, events, or locales is entirely coincidental.

Cover Design: Stephanie Gaston

www.FrightVisionBooks.com

Facebook: @FrightVisionBooks

Dearest Visitor,

Welcome!

Sometimes your mind makes you think one thing, but reality is something completely different.

Enjoy the ride, perhaps it is what you expected all along, but perhaps not.

Your nightmare is ready. Let's begin!

Sweetest Dreams,

Crantz

CHAPTER ONE

Josh was in the middle of watching his favorite gamer Let's Play Video. "Hurry up, Josh. I want you to take these cookies while they're still hot."

Ugh. Josh tried pretending that he couldn't hear his mom calling, but she was on to him.

"You've always told me not to talk to strangers. Sorry, Mom, I don't think it's safe," he said—half as a joke, half hoping she'd fall for the excuse.

"The Waters aren't strangers; they're your new neighbors. It's hard moving to a new place. We need to show them that they are welcome. Come on, Josh. Just go take them the basket and tell them that we're here if they need anything."

"Can't you do it? They'd rather talk to you anyway."

"No. I've got work I need to finish. And besides, I think it'll be good for you to go introduce yourself and meet new people. You're always so glued to your phone."

Josh grumbled that he met plenty of people online who actually liked the same stuff he did. His mom wasn't having it. It was time to admit defeat. Slowly, he got up and put on his shoes. They were too big and he felt like he was wearing clown shoes every time he put them on. His dad always bought him clothes that were at least one size too big, "to give him room to grow." Maybe he could spend the summer cutting grass for some of his neighbors. Then he'd be able to buy his own clothes for school next year.

He sighed and checked the mirror in the hallway. His blonde hair was a complete mess. He tried to push it down flat against his head, but it just made things worse and he gave up. At least he was wearing his go to t-shirt that featured his favorite video game character, who had messy blond hair just like Josh, and carried a shining sword and shield. Josh grabbed the basket of oatmeal cookies–*I thought mom wanted to make a* good *impression, blah!*—and headed next door.

It was good that someone had finally bought that old place. It was a nice house, with a small front porch that had white columns on either side. But it had been sitting empty for so long that the pale blue paint was starting to turn grey and peel, and the trees and bushes sat wildly overgrown. As he climbed the steps, he couldn't help but notice that the door was ajar. The neighbors must have left it open while they were unpacking. Just as he was reaching out to knock on it, the wind picked up, and the door swung open, as if inviting him in.

"Hello?" Josh called. No one answered.

He stuck his head in to see if anyone was around. The place was empty. All he could see were boxes stacked to the ceiling. Each one was labeled with its final destination. Living room. Kitchen. Bedroom. Only one box had been opened. It looked worn and older than the other boxes, and it was the only one without a label on it.

Surely with the door being left open, someone had to be here.

"Is anyone home?" Josh called out. Still, no response. Slowly, he started inching his way inside, craning to see if maybe someone was upstairs.

As he got closer though, he couldn't help but take a peek into the opened box. It seemed to be filled with odds and ends for house decorating. In it he could see a few little statues and figurines like he had seen displayed in his grandmother's glass cabinets. But they weren't nearly as cute as his grandmother's baby angel collection. These looked like something from a monster movie.

There was one figurine of a woman with three heads who was holding a snake like a baby. A big ugly cyclops with one eye was lying next to her. There was a centaur with the body of a horse and the head of a man. And, weirdest of all, a skull wearing a purple top hat.

Josh figured this family must be into some kind of role-playing games and decided to dig deeper to see what other kinds of cool games they might have. Maybe if they had the same game sets, they could all play together! Surely just a little peeking wouldn't hurt. Besides, no one was around anyway. He set the basket of cookies down and started rummaging. But instead of board games, he found some dried flowers and a couple of jars filled with spices and liquids. Josh made a face when he saw one was full of pickled pigs feet. Under all of that were plain black and white curtains or table cloths, Josh couldn't tell which. Lifting the fabric revealed a stack of books with strange writing on them. They looked old and smelled of leather. There didn't seem to be any more game stuff in here and he was just about to give up when something glistening in gold at the bottom caught his eye. Curious, he grabbed the item and pulled it out from the bottom of the box. Holding it up, he could see that it was a gold framed picture of a girl that looked to be about the same age as him. She was really pretty too with a little button nose, sparkling blue eyes, and a big bow in her curly blonde hair.

"Hello!"

"YUARGH!" He jumped, trying to hide the picture behind his back and knocked over the basket with his foot, spilling cookies everywhere. Instinctively, he jammed the frame into his cargo pocket.

A girl appeared in front of him. He must not have seen her between all of the boxes that were piled up. Once his heart stopped pounding from the shock, he realized that it was the same exact girl from the picture. And she was even prettier in person.

Way to go, Mr. Smooth, he thought to himself. Here he is, lucky enough to have this girl moving in right next door, and the first time they meet she catches him breaking into their house and going through their stuff.

To make matters worse, he had just screamed and almost wet his pants in front of her. It almost made him mad how cute she was with her nose wrinkling and her curly hair bouncing as she giggled at him.

Josh could feel his face turning a bright shade of red. "My parents wanted me to bring those over," he mumbled, desperate to get out of there.

"Don't worry about the mess, my mom will clean it up," she reassured him. "My name is Beatrice," she said, thankfully changing the subject.

"I'm Josh," he replied.

"Hi Josh," she smiled. She looked as though she was just about to say something else, but instead exclaimed, "Ah! I love that game!"

"Huh?" Josh was confused at first. But then he followed her gaze. "Oh, my shirt! Yeah, this is from the original game. I absolutely love it!" he said grinning from ear to ear.

"What level did you get to?" She asked, bouncing with excitement.

"Level 12," he said with a smirk, glad that he could brag about his high score. There was no way this girl could beat that!

"Ah-ha! I've gotten to level 14!"

"No way!"

"Yup!"

"Well I guess you'll just have to prove it to me sometime," he said, crossing his arms.

"Oh, you are so on!" she said, taunting him and giggling. Suddenly her smile dropped. "But I don't know when. I can't seem to find any of my stuff lately," she said with a sigh. "It's so frustrating. I don't know what my parents have done with everything."

"Maybe they sold it all so they could afford to buy a bigger house." Josh joked, trying to impress her with his amazing humor. She just stared at him, while he stood frozen with a dumb smirk on his face.

"At this point I wouldn't be surprised. I can't find any of my stuff. Here, I'll show you what I mean. The upstairs is completely empty."

Did she really want to take him upstairs? Josh wasn't sure what to do. He knew he was just getting a tour of the house, but it felt weird to go upstairs with a girl that he hardly knew when no one else was home.

Unsure what to do, he slowly followed her up the stairs, and she led him into an empty room with a big window that was set off in a little cubby that could be perfect for a cozy window seat. "See, this is supposed to be my room and none of my stuff is here. I don't even have a bed!" she frowned.

"Don't worry, I'm sure your parents will get your room all set up in no time. They just have to go through all the boxes first."

"All of those ugly boxes. I don't know what my parents are planning to do with everything, but I really don't like how they've packed everything up."

Josh wasn't sure what to say. He could imagine how hard it must be to have to pick up your whole life and move to a new place where you didn't know anyone. And he would be frustrated too, if his parents packed his stuff and he couldn't find any of it. At the same time, he knew that her parents would be getting everything in place as fast as they could. After all, they'd just moved in, and unpacking would take a little while.

He gave her a sympathetic look, "How about we go downstairs and I'll help you look through the boxes for your stuff?"

Beatrice smiled, "That would be great!"

They made their way back down the stairs, but just as they got to the bottom, he heard people walking up to the front door.

"My parents will be upset if they know that we've been here alone together! Go!" Beatrice whispered to him.

"Okay, I'll be back tomorrow!" he promised her. Then he quickly ran out the back door, just barely missing her parents.

As he sneaked around the corner of the house, he peaked in and saw them from the window. Her parents seemed furious about the mess from the cookies and all the things he'd taken out of the box. He could see Beatrice trying to explain, but they looked like they were just ignoring her. He should have just cleaned up the mess instead of leaving it there. What had he been thinking?

He continued to watch as Mrs. Waters went over to the open box and began flailing her arms and pointing. Josh looked down at his bulging cargo pocket. The picture! It was still in his pocket. He had forgotten to put it back. Mrs. Waters must have noticed it was missing, and she was really upset. He felt bad, but it was too late to put it back. And besides, now he had a picture of Beatrice. Shrugging and smiling, he decided to keep it.

CHAPTER TWO

The next day at school, Josh couldn't wait to tell his friends all about the new girl next door. When the time came for lunch, he rushed over to find Tom and Clio already at their usual table.

Tom had his earbuds in, as he always did. He was probably watching one of his favorite video channels about some sort of alien conspiracy theory. Tom loved all the wild stories on the internet, and he spent most of his time learning about them. Josh was pretty sure that if aliens were real, Tom must be one. After all, he was the craziest—and smartest—kid Josh knew.

Clio, on the other hand, was busy multitasking. She seemed to be building a sandwich, texting, and finishing homework all at the same time. Her dark braids swished around her as she quickly went from one activity to the other. She was so serious and focused that it would have been easy to mistake her for a teacher if it weren't for her size. Even though she was a bit older than either Josh or Tom, she was still the shortest. Josh thought that she might be trying to make up for her lack of a growth spurt by always trying to show how mature she was.

Josh had been best friends with them both since kindergarten. There was no one else in the world Josh could count on like these two.

"Guys, I have big news!" Josh announced.

Tom took an earbud out and glanced up, adjusting the glasses on his freckled face. Clio raised her eyebrows.

"A new family just moved in next to my house. And they have a girl who's our age!" Josh exclaimed.

"So what? There are plenty of other kids that live in *my* neighborhood. Kids live everywhere," Clio said.

Josh rolled his eyes.

"Do you know what classes she has?" Tom asked.

"I'm not sure," Josh replied. He hoped to run into her in the hallways, or see her in one of his classes. It would be exciting if it turned out they had some of the same classes together! He made a mental note to ask her about her schedule the next time that he saw her. "I'll try to find out," he added.

"Tell us more about her. Where is she from? There are big craters located in certain areas of the world that are fool-proof evidence of the Alien Space War! Maybe she's seen it for herself! I'd love to interview her about her experience there," Tom was going on about his theories again.

Josh chuckled. "I don't know where she's from or if she knows anything about the Alien Space War, but maybe!" Josh replied with a grin.

"I haven't heard anything about a new girl in school," said Clio. "Shouldn't she be enrolling today? I know my dad would get me in school as fast as possible if we moved. He doesn't think kids should miss a day unless they are so sick that they're in the hospital."

"Oh! I bet her whole family has to meet with a CIA agent to get their cover stories so they can start a new life. I bet they found out too much about the alien war and they're part of a witness relocation program to make sure they don't get abducted!" Tom sounded both excited and nervous as he looked over his shoulder. Josh could only assume he was either worried a CIA agent would overhear him or he was afraid that one of the teachers was secretly an alien and he had just blown the Waters family's cover.

"Maybe," Josh said. Tom got picked on enough for his crazy ideas so Josh tried to appease him. "But I kinda think that they're probably just getting settled in. I'm sure they'll bring her to school sometime this week to get her all set up."

"Well when she does get here, try not to drool on your books. Other kids will have to use them after you, you know." Clio tried to sound like she was teasing, but Josh thought he heard a hint of jealousy in her voice.

He tried to give her a nasty look, but he couldn't help but laugh. Clio liked to take herself so seriously these days, but deep down she was still the same dork he'd always known.

Josh decided that he would try to go see Beatrice as soon as school was over. Seeing her again was all he could think about as his afternoon classes dragged. Especially Mr. Robinson's history class. He almost fell asleep while Mr. Robinson droned on and on about some archaeology site he'd volunteered at and how they had just dug up an ancient toilet. The only reason Josh was still awake was because Tom had grabbed his shoulder to tell him that he'd seen a video online that showed how alien eggs are often mistaken for dried poo, and that when they hatched, the space larvae would take a human host and eat him alive from the inside.

Finally, the bell rang and Josh was free! As soon as he got home, he threw his books in his room and went to the bathroom to make sure he looked okay. He was proud of his new t-shirt that had an elf from the video game that he and Beatrice talked about on the front holding a sword and shield. He thought it'd make for another good conversation starter. Josh ran a comb through his hair, took a deep breath, and left for Beatrice's house.

As he walked up the path to her door he got more and more nervous. All Josh had been able to think about was how excited he was to see Beatrice again. He'd forgotten all about how angry her parents were when they came home and saw the mess he'd made.

Shakily, he made his way up the porch steps. His heart was pounding. He rang the bell thinking about what he'd say to Beatrice when she opened the door. But it wasn't Beatrice that answered. Mrs. Waters, a short woman with the same small nose as Beatrice, opened it instead.

"Hi. Uh, you must be Beatrice's parents. I'm … Josh. From, umm, next door. Is Beatrice … where is she?" Josh fumbled with his words, having been surprised when the person at the door wasn't Beatrice.

Mrs. Waters gasped and scowled at Josh. Her eyes looked wild.

"Where is it? I know you took it!" She shouted. So she knew he took the picture! Josh stumbled backwards and could barely breathe; he was so scared. But it was when she dropped her voice and growled softly at him that he started to know real terror. "If you don't give it back to me now, I swear you will regret it. I will make you wish you'd never stepped foot in this house, you ugly clown-footed thief." Oh no, It was just a little picture, how could she be this upset? Josh didn't mean for it to be such a big deal. Suddenly her voiced dropped very low and she leaned in so close to Josh that he could feel her hot breath on his face. "You have no idea what I'm capable of," she growled.

Just then, Mr. Waters grabbed her and closed the door.

Josh stood there for a moment trying to figure out what to do next. Trembling, he started to turn and leave when the door opened again. Nervous, Josh turned only to see Mr. Waters' big body taking up the whole door. He was a tall man with broad shoulders and a thick black beard. Put him in a fancy coat and an ugly sailboat and he could have been a mean pirate. The look on his face was so angry and serious that Josh's smile instantly vanished. Shaking, Josh realized how stupid he had been to come here.

"Do you think this is funny?" Mr. Waters boomed. Josh didn't know what he was talking about, but he shook his head quickly, not wanting to anger him any more than he already was. "Can't you see the trouble that you're causing? My wife is losing her mind with grief and you show up and steal the only things she has left! You're lucky we don't call the police. Now get out of here and stop with the games, boy!"

Josh didn't wait long enough to answer. He turned and ran straight back to his house all the way to his room. Panting, he slammed his bedroom door and leaned against it to catch his breath. He pulled out his phone and texted Tom and Clio.

CHAPTER THREE

Josh: Guys I think im in trouble… o_0

Clio: Why?

Josh: Well I went over the Waters…

Clio: I knew it had something to do with that girl! >:(

Josh: yeah well they're really mad at me. DX

Tom: I told u they were keeping secrets! That y they r so mad becuz they know u r onto them. :O

Josh: I think u might be right about the secrets thing Tom

Clio: What do you mean? What happened?

Josh: Well I kinda stole a picture from their house… :/

Tom: 0_0

Clio: You WHAT?!?! :O If my dad finds out about this…

Tom: Her dads a policeman! :o

*Josh: I KNOW THAT TOM! Clio, Pls dont tell him! _/|_*

Clio: I won't. But this new girl stuff has got to stop.

Josh: Ok but Mr. Waters said something rly weird when he was yelling at me

Tom: wat did he say?????

Josh: he said that I was stealing 1 of the only things they have left :/

Clio: Only thing left of what?

Tom: It must be all they have left from the space craft!!!!!!!

Clio: Maybe he just meant because they lost a lot of things when they moved

Josh: Idk. whatevr it is ive nvr seen anyone so mad :(

Clio: Well you did break into their house >:(

Josh: he also said they were grieving …

Just then, Josh's mom called him for dinner.

Josh: gotta go. Dinner time. ttyl

At the dinner table, Josh decided to ask his parents what they knew about the Waters family.

"Nothing much, son. They' just moved here, we haven't had a chance to find out about them," Josh's dad replied.

"But I still haven't seen Beatrice at school," Josh said.

"Who's Beatrice?" his mom asked.

"The Waters' daughter," Josh replied.

Both parents gave each other a strange look. "Son, the Waters don't have a daughter," his dad said.

"What? But I—"

"I don't know what you may have heard, but I can tell you that Mr. and Mrs. Waters don't have any kids, Josh. You should just leave it at that," his mom said.

But Josh knew that the Waters had a daughter. After all, he had seen her and even met her, for crying out loud! And why wouldn't his parents even talk about it. It was like they knew something they didn't want to tell him. Something was definitely off.

That night as Josh lay in bed, he found himself staring at the picture of Beatrice. He couldn't believe that one picture in such a simple frame could be the cause of so much trouble. He didn't mean to steal it. He hadn't even realized it was still in his pocket until he was already outside. He'd just been so startled when Beatrice jumped out at him that he'd forgotten he was holding it. And now, that simple mistake had her dad yelling at him and her mom threatening him.

As scary as her dad had been, it really was her mom that truly terrified him.

I mean, he thought to himself, *what kind of grown up threatens a kid like she did? And she made fun of my feet!*

He looked down angrily and kicked his shoes off so that they went flying across the room. He sat steaming, thinking of all the things he wished he'd said back to her. *Well I'd rather have big clown feet than be able to play connect the dots with all the moles on my face!* Or: *At least I'm tall enough to ride all the rides at the carnival, shorty!* Or maybe: *What's that? I couldn't hear you over smell of your breath!* Then he would have walked away, leaving her there with her mouth open in shock. And just as she was about to say something else, he would have made a rude gesture and kept on walking. Ha! That would have shown her!

But he hadn't done any of that. He'd just stood there shaking.

Frustrated with himself, he rolled over and propped Beatrice's picture up on his bed against the wall. He started drifting off. *I'm such a coward,* he thought.

Through the fog of sleep he could swear he heard Beatrice's voice, "You're not a coward. Mom can be really scary when she's mad."

*　　　*　　　*

"Guys, something isn't right. I asked my parents about Beatrice last night and they said the Waters don't have any children," Josh said the next day at the lunch table.

Clio scowled at him. "I seriously cannot believe that you broke in and stole something from those people."

"I know. I'll give it back to them, okay. But what about their secret? Why would the Waters be saying weird stuff like that? And why are my parents trying to tell me they don't have any kids? Something just isn't right."

"Well, I was doing some research last night. I think I was wrong about Beatrice being involved with aliens," Tom said.

Josh looked at him, surprised. Once Tom got an idea in his head he never changed his mind.

"So you are ready to let go of your alien obsession now?" Clio asked, a little too roughly, Josh thought.

"I'm not saying aliens might not be involved," Tom said, sounding hurt. "But I was watching this video last night about a haunted snow globe. See, this guy had this snow globe from New York and he took it with him to the top of the Statue of Liberty. He was holding it up so he could take a picture of it with New York City behind it, because it was the city inside the globe! But just as he did, the Statue was struck by lightning! He got hit with a bazillion volts of electricity. All that was left of him was the snow globe and four eyelashes. And now, anyone who touches the snow globe can see him, still standing at the top of the Statue of Liberty looking at all the tall buildings."

"Okay ... so what's your point?" Clio asked, with a raised eyebrow.

"Well," Tom said, looking much less sure of himself than usual, "Josh said that his parents were acting weird when he asked about Beatrice, and that they told him the Waters didn't have a kid. And when her dad was yelling at him, he said that they were grieving, right? And her mom was freaking out about losing the picture. What if that picture is like the snow globe? What if Beatrice is a ghost and that picture is how her mom talks to her?"

"That's it, I'm going to go sit somewhere else," Clio announced. "I'll meet you guys after school for the project." She picked up her tray and left. She had clearly had enough of Tom's nonsense.

But, Josh felt goosebumps on the back of his neck while Tom was talking. There was no way that Beatrice could be a ghost, that didn't make any more sense than her being an alien from some other galaxy. After all, Josh had met her and she sure didn't look like a ghost. Wouldn't he have been able to tell? Weren't ghosts supposed to be spooky and transparent, gliding through walls and making the room cold? None of this had happened with Beatrice. But what if Tom was right?

"Do you really think," Josh said, reaching into his bag and pulling out the picture, "that this could be like the snow globe and somehow let us talk to a ghost?" It could explain everything. Sure, sometimes Tom had some outlandish ideas, but he was a smart kid, and he wasn't crazy.

"It would probably make more sense if you saw the video," Tom said, taking the picture. "But my parents took away my phone last night after I put salt in their coffee. Slug people can change shape and look like anyone! I just wanted to make sure that Mom and Dad hadn't been encased in slime and replaced by slug look alikes! I saw a video that said the slug people really like to kidnap dentists, and you know Dad's a dentist!"

Josh sat there for a full minute with his mouth open. Nope, he was wrong. Tom was crazy.

CHAPTER FOUR

That Friday afternoon, Josh and Tom walked off the bus together with Clio not far behind them. Mr. Robinson had given them the fun assignment of creating a diorama of the Trojan Horse. It took half an hour for Clio and Josh to convince Tom that they didn't need to make the Trojan Horse fully robotic. He was sure that the Trojans had had superior technology, but carefully hid it from the rest of the world. It came to them from secret vaults of ancient knowledge given to the people of Atlantis by their alien allies. The only reason he finally agreed to a simple stick figure was because Josh pointed out that a robot would take so long to build that he wouldn't have any time left to play his new video game that weekend.

As they all glued popsicle sticks together for the horse, Josh couldn't help but steal glances out the window over at the Waters' house. He had to know what was going on over there and what had happened to Beatrice.

"Alright, I don't think we can do much else to this horse until the glue dries," Clio said, closing the caps on the glue bottles. "What should we do while we wait?"

"A new season of Alien Life Forms just came out. We could all watch that!" Tom suggested.

"Or … we could all go over and see Beatrice," Josh said.

"What? We can't do that!" Clio said. "You'll just get in trouble with her parents again."

"They just left," he said with a mischievous grin. "You can see their driveway from the window, and I bet Beatrice is home by herself."

"Yeah, let's go over and find out what's going on!" Tom ran to the window as the Waters' car turned onto the street.

"You guys, this is ridiculous. If you're going, I'm not coming with you," Clio huffed with her hand on her hip.

"Come on, Clio," Josh begged. "Don't you want to meet Beatrice and finally be able to know the truth?" She didn't look impressed.

"Well if you don't want to come for yourself, why don't you come for us—you know we're just going to get ourselves into more trouble without you there to help us." Josh knew she couldn't resist feeling like she was the mature one. Let her think whatever she wanted if it meant that she would come with them.

"Ugh. Fine. But only because I can't trust you two not to steal something else or end up in jail this time." She said with a satisfied look on her face.

As they made their way over to the Waters' house, Josh was so glad he had his two best friends by his side in all of this, even if Clio thought it was all ridiculous. Weird things were going on, and it was scary to face them by himself.

Before they reached the house, Tom stopped, pulling Josh to the side. "Here," he said as he pulled out a small green bottle. It had an alien sticker on it with a big red "X" drawn over it. "Alien repellent so we don't have to worry about getting abducted," he explained. And before Josh could argue, he was being sprayed all over.

"Nuh-uh!" Clio exclaimed before Tom had the chance to do the same to her.

"Come on, Clio, it will keep you safe!" Tom insisted.

"I thought you said this isn't about aliens," she said, squinting through the stink coming off of Josh.

"Well, I don't think it is, but you can never be too careful!" Tom said with a very serious look on his face as he began to spray himself from head to foot.

"Yuck! What is this stuff made of?" Josh coughed. "It smells like rotten fruit and armpit!"

"Oh just some lemon juice, garlic, salt, and curry powder!"

"Ewww! Is this really necessary?" Josh smelled so disgusting that he almost hoped Beatrice wouldn't be there. He could imagine how embarrassing it would be for Beatrice to smell him with that nasty spray all over him. Why did Tom have to go to extremes like this?

"Yes!" Tom replied. "Do you want to be taken to Mars and have your ear canals probed? I guess Clio wouldn't mind it, since she's not got anything in her head anyway," he said, sticking his tongue out at her.

Josh decided to just shake it off. After all, there was nothing he could do about Tom's foolishness now anyway. Beatrice could be in trouble; she might need him. He had to do this.

They made their way to the porch. Tom and Clio stayed at the bottom of the steps, just like they'd planned. Josh was dreading what he was about to face. He closed his eyes and took a deep breath. Hesitantly, with every ounce of courage he could gather, Josh knocked on the door.

They waited.

A few seconds went by, but to Josh, they felt like hours. A bead of sweat formed on his temple.

He knocked again. There was still no answer.

Josh wasn't sure what to do. His heart was racing and he looked back to Tom and Clio for ideas.

Tom was standing with his head tilted to one side and a strange look on his face. "Do you hear that?" he asked.

Josh was not in the mood for any of Tom's nonsense right now. He was about to turn and leave when he heard it too. A soft whimper like a little girl crying.

"Yeah!" Josh said, full of excitement, "It seems to be coming from inside the house!"

"What are you two talking about? I don't hear anything," Clio said with a confused look on her face.

They all listened for a moment, and to Josh and Tom it was clear that someone was crying. They looked at each other with a mix of fear and excitement and ran over to the window to see what was happening. Clio was slow to follow them. She just kept looking at them like she thought they had lost their minds.

"Look!" Tom pointed. Josh's face lit up when he peered inside. There, sitting at the top of the steps was Beatrice with hair pulled back into a ponytail and her head on her knees. He was so glad to see her again! She must not have heard him knocking on the door. Suddenly, he realized she was the one that was crying. That made him even more worried than before. He went back to the door and rang the bell this time, hoping she would hear it.

"W-who's there?" Beatrice's small voice stuttered.

"It's me, Josh," he replied.

"You shouldn't be here. My parents will be really mad if they find out," she said through sniffles. He could hardly hear her through the door.

"It's hard for me to hear you. Can you let me in, just for a few minutes?" he asked.

"I can't. My parents will be back soon," she responded.

"Okay, then how about we talk at the window?" he said as he walked over to the nearest one. He pushed Tom out of the way so he could see her better.

Beatrice sat there for a minute, seeming to decide what to do. Finally, he saw her stand up and start gliding down the stairs.

"You didn't tell me she had big ears," Tom hissed angrily. "That changes everything! It's not aliens OR ghosts! It must be the Lizard People! They're so self-conscious because lizards don't even *have* ears that they always choose victims with really big ones!"

"Shut up!" Josh growled. He was starting to regret bringing Tom along after all. He looked back through the window and saw Beatrice peeking through the curtains, giving Tom a strange look. Josh was mortified, she must have overheard him!

"Who are they?" she asked, looking at Tom, then over at Clio.

"Hi! I'm Tom!" Tom practically yelled. "I brought you some alien repellant, but now I don't guess that will help!

Josh's eyes got real big and he could feel his face getting hotter and hotter. He looked directly at Beatrice and mouthed the words "He's crazy" to her, mostly to try to save himself. Beatrice was probably thinking that Josh must be as crazy as Tom just for hanging out with him.

"It's okay," she said, giggling and wiping away tears. "I'm just glad to talk to someone else. Ever since you came over the other day, my parents won't even talk to me. They're completely ignoring me, like I'm not even here." She began to sob again, "I'm just so lonely."

Josh wasn't sure what to do. Could all of this really be his fault somehow?

"Listen," he said, "I'm so sorry I got you into all this trouble. I think they're mad at me because I—"

"They're here! HIDE!" Clio cried, before he could finish his sentence.

They turned and saw Beatrice's parents pulling into the driveway. They were terrified. Maybe they hadn't seen them because of the bushes that were overgrown around the porch! They looked at each other and knew they had to move.

All three dove from the porch and hit the ground—hard. Josh struggled not to yell when he felt his ribs bash into the earth. They all laid very still, afraid to even breathe.

CHAPTER FIVE

"I don't know what's happened to her. We have to get it back!" They heard Mrs. Waters say as they got out of the car.

"Maybe we shouldn't have done it in the first place. Look at all the trouble it's caused. I warned you," Mr. Waters countered.

"Trouble? The only thing causing trouble is that snooping Martin boy stealing my daughter!" Mrs. Waters practically yelled. Martin boy? They were talking about Josh! Josh thought this was a bit extreme for her to say though. He didn't steal her daughter ... just the picture. What could she possibly mean?

"No, I think this has gone way too far, Lisa."

"You don't understand!" she snapped.

"I miss her as much as you do, but this isn't healthy. We need to come to terms with the fact that Beatrice is gone."

Mr. Waters was trying to unlock the door while balancing grocery bags in his arms. "We have to put an end to this," he said gravely, as the door closed behind him.

Josh, Tom, and Clio all exchanged scared glances as they laid there, still afraid to move. What did he mean that Beatrice was gone? What had they done?

The Waters came out again to get more bags, and they could hear Mrs. Waters yelling, "Absolutely not! We agreed this is how we're going to save her!"

"Lisa, it's too dangerous—"

"I said no." Mrs. Waters turned on Mr. Waters with a quiet fury that made all their hair stand on end. "You don't want to cross me, John. You know what I'm capable of."

"Yes, I do." Mr. Waters said. He sounded like he was seeing her for the first time. "Now I do."

"Good." Her voice was ice. "Get the rest of the bags. I'm going inside to search for that boy. We are getting the picture back. We're going to find her, no matter what it takes."

BAM!

Josh thought he'd been shot! But it was just the door slamming behind Mrs. Waters. Josh was completely frozen in fear as he heard Mr. Waters follow her in and lock all the locks inside the house.

"I can't believe what we just heard," Josh panted.

"Me neither," Tom said, looking at him wide-eyed. "I don't care if they're aliens or Lizard People, it sounds like she's coming after you."

"We've got to get out of here!" Josh whispered. He slowly poked his head over the side of the porch to make sure the coast was clear. He didn't see anyone. Beatrice was no longer by the window. She must have left when her parents came back. He gestured to Tom and Clio, and the three of them crawled to the edge of the house. After one more look around to make sure no one was watching, they tore off as fast as they could, running for the safety of Josh's house. As they ran, Josh could have sworn they heard Mrs. Waters screaming and chanting.

When they got to his room, Josh paced with nervous energy. Tom was practically jumping up and down with excitement—it was all like the stories he watched online! Clio collapsed against the wall and slid down to the floor. Her eyes stared blankly ahead.

"Who's going to talk first?" Tom asked, looking from Josh to Clio to Josh again.

"I'm dead," Josh said numbly. His stomach began to feel queasy as he thought about Mrs. Waters' threats. Now he really wished Tom hadn't sprayed him with that awful stuff—the smell was making him even more nauseated.

"What are you talking about?" Tom looked at him confused. "You're not dead, dummy. Beatrice is!"

"Tom, this isn't the time for your stupid theories, OK. They think I've done something to Beatrice and they said they're coming after me!"

"Well yeah, because you took her snow globe," Tom said.

"Stop it, Tom! This isn't funny anymore! Every day I have to listen to your crazy stories. Even when everyone else is laughing at you, or thinks you're crazy, or avoids you, I'm always there, because we've been friends forever. But this is too much! Either stop and actually help me, or just go. I don't need this." Josh was so angry that he'd turned red and was breathing heavy.

Tom's face fell, and his shoulders slumped as all of his energy gave out and he crumpled onto the bed. "I'm just trying to help," he said in a small, beaten-down voice. "I mean, didn't you hear them? They said that Beatrice was gone. And that they lost her when you took the picture."

Josh was shaking with fury. "This stupid picture," he yelled, as he pulled it out of his backpack and waved it in Tom's face, "has been nothing but trouble. But that's because I *stole* it, not because it's some kind of ghost antenna like you saw online." He tossed the picture into the corner with a snarl. "This is the real world, Tom. You're too old for this. I'm in trouble because I messed up, and now I have real grown up people who want to hurt me. This is serious!"

Tom sat with his eyes glued to the floor. Even through his anger, Josh couldn't help but feel bad when a shiny trail made its way down Tom's cheek. He could feel the rage draining and he wanted to reach out to him. But as much as he wanted to be a good friend to Tom, enough was enough. He was in real trouble and he needed real help. Thankfully, he still had Clio.

Suddenly, he realized how quiet she had been. She hadn't said anything the whole time they were at Beatrice's house. And all she'd done since they'd gotten back to his room was stare out the window.

"Clio?" he said. She sat there with her vacant expression. "Are you okay?" he asked.

Slowly, Clio tried to speak, but her voice caught. She licked her lips and cleared her throat. Still looking through the window, she said, "Who were you two talking to before Mr. and Mrs. Waters came home?"

Tom looked up, his eyes still glistening.

"You mean Beatrice?" Josh asked, very confused.

"There was no one there, Josh," she said in a hollow voice.

"What do you mean 'No one was there'? Beatrice was standing at the window. How could you not see her, you were right there beside me," he said. "Tom, you saw her, didn't you?"

Tom's eyes grew bigger. "Yeah, I saw her," he said.

"Well I looked through the window. I saw all the boxes and furniture, but I didn't see a girl. I didn't see anyone at all. The house was empty." Clio started to push herself up from the floor, never taking her eyes off the window.

"I don't understand what you're saying, Clio. Beatrice was literally standing right in front of the window. How could you miss her?" Josh asked, starting to feel frustrated again.

She moved across the room to the window. Josh realized that she hadn't been just staring off into space that whole time. She was looking across at the Waters' house.

"That's it!" Tom said excitedly, jumping up and rushing to her side.

"I've been sitting here trying to make sense of everything. Her parents being so mad about the picture. Them saying she was gone. Their threats. And you two, talking into an empty window. But I couldn't figure out a logical reason. I just keep seeing the curtains in that window blowing around. But the window is closed," Clio said. Josh was starting to worry that the stress and shock from earlier had short-circuited her brain.

She reached a hand out. "Tom," she said, not even blinking as she stared at the moving curtains, "hand me the picture."

Tom slid the frame into her hand. She looked from the photo to the window and back again, and they watched as her eyes grew larger.

"I don't believe it," Clio gasped.

CHAPTER SIX

Clio stared open-mouthed at the golden-haired girl in the window next door. Beatrice waved at Tom and Clio. Clio raised a shaking arm and waved back, while Tom bounced on his spot laughing. "This can't be happening," she muttered out of the corner of her mouth.

Josh still didn't fully understand. "What are you talking about?" He stomped over to the window and looked out. Even in his bad mood, he couldn't help but smile when he saw Beatrice. He felt his face flush when she smiled back.

"Hey! Open your window," Tom yelled across the expanse of yard between the two houses, "so we can all talk!"

Clio jumped and put her hand over Tom's mouth. They could see Beatrice looking for a way to open the window, as the porch light came on at her house and Mrs. Waters came flying out and looking in their direction. The three of them dove to the floor.

"Be quiet!" Josh hissed, "What are you thinking?"

"Now that we know she's a ghost, I thought maybe we could talk to her and find out about the great beyond." Tom looked surprised at their reactions.

"We're already in enough trouble! And I told you to stop with the ghost stories!" Josh felt his anger rising again.

"No," Clio said, looking straight into Josh's eyes. "I think Tom is right about Beatrice."

Josh felt his body going limp. The emotional roller coaster of the past few hours was just too much for him. He couldn't believe his ears. He sat, feeling pale and confused.

"I'm serious," Clio said. "When I was looking at that window before, there was no one there. I swear. But as soon as I touched her picture, Beatrice appeared out of nowhere—she just popped into place like she'd been there the whole time. As crazy as it sounds, Tom is right. Somehow this picture is a link between her ghost and the world of the living."

Josh's eyes moved from Clio's serious face to Tom's, who was looking back at him with a big grin and one raised eyebrow that said *I told you so*.

"Clio," Josh began, not sure what to say, "there has to be some other explanation."

"There's not. I've been over it and over it in my head. How else can you explain how she just appeared for me? And it would explain why the Waters are so mad. When you took the picture you took away their link to Beatrice. I bet they can't see her anymore."

Josh's eyes widened. "Beatrice said that they were ignoring her and acting like she wasn't around. I thought it was just because they were mad. Are you saying it's because they couldn't actually see her?"

"Yes! See, it all makes sense," Clio said. Despite the certainty in her voice, she looked just as shocked as Josh felt.

"The question," Tom said, suddenly sitting up and looking concerned, "is whether her parents know or not."

"What do you mean?" Clio asked.

"Well, think about it. If they don't know that she's a ghost, then their daughter just disappeared," Tom replied.

Clio looked skeptical. "But then they would have gone to the police or been out looking for her," she replied. Josh could see the wheels turning in her head. He never thought he'd witness Clio and Tom working together on a conspiracy theory.

"Exactly!" Tom said. "That must mean they knew about the picture and Beatrice's ghost! I've heard that these types of objects can be made by someone who knows the right spells."

"Whoa." Josh's head was starting to hurt. "Ghosts? OK. Crazy mom's threatening to hurt me? Sure. But now you want us to believe that the Waters know magic and somehow bound Beatrice's ghost to this picture on purpose? Clio, you can't believe this."

"Actually, that makes a lot of sense. That's the last piece of the puzzle," she said, clearly impressed with Tom's knowledge.

Josh felt like the whole world had gone crazy. "This is insa—"

KNOCK! KNOCK! KNOCK!

The three of them jumped at the loud sound and scattered about the room to try to assume normal positions.

"Just a minute!" Josh cried.

"Now!" His father's voice boomed back at him.

Quickly, Clio slid the picture under Josh's pillow while he went to answer the door. Josh's dad stood there looking angrier than Josh had ever seen him. Josh tried to remember if he'd forgotten to do some chores or something—why was his dad so mad? But then he saw a tall, stern-looking police officer behind his dad.

For a split second, Josh thought about running. But his dad was blocking the door, and his room was on the second story, so he couldn't jump out the window. He was going to face his time in jail like a man.

He was about to say that he'd tell them everything when he heard Clio's voice ring out.

"Dad?" she said with confusion in her voice. So many things were going through Josh's mind. Of course this was Clio's dad! Josh had always known he was a policeman, but he'd never met him before. Maybe he was here to pick her up! But then why did he look so angry?

"Kids, Officer Jones needs to talk to you," Josh's dad said, still looking daggers into his son.

Clio's dad invited himself into Josh's room, closing the door behind him.

Oh thank goodness, he only wanted to talk. Josh tried to calm himself down a bit, but he was sure that everyone else in the room could hear his heart beating against his ribcage too.

"What's going on, Dad?" Clio asked calmly.

With a huff, he sat down on the bed beside Clio, making the pillow that hid the picture shift a bit. Josh watched as Clio tried to smoothly push the picture further back to keep her dad from finding it.

Tom still stood near the window, frozen and wide-eyed.

"Have a seat, boys," Clio's dad commanded. They obeyed. Josh turned his desk chair around to face Officer Jones. Tom sat straight down where he had been standing.

"I am very disappointed in all of you, but especially you, Clio," he said, glaring at his daughter. "I know I've raised you better. I have a report that you three have been harassing the Waters family."

"No we weren't," Clio started.

"Then why were you yelling at them from your window? And don't try to say that you didn't. Mrs. Waters may have called the police, but Josh's parents heard you too."

Dangit Tom! Josh thought. For a kid who was so smart, Tom could be so dumb sometimes!

"You're just lucky that I'm the one who heard the call today, or else you might have had a much meaner policeman show up to take care of you three."

"But the Waters are the ones keeping secrets!" Tom blurted. Both Josh and Clio shot him a look, but Tom was oblivious. "We saw Beatrice! We know what's going on!"

"How do you know about that?" Clio's dad asked, his eyes narrowing.

"We saw her with the picture!"

"Tom!" Josh finally yelled. He was saying too much; he was going to get them in even more trouble than they already were!

"Ah, yes. The picture." He turned to stare squarely at Josh. "Care to tell me why the Waters believe that you broke into their house when they first moved in? And that you stole a picture of their daughter?"

Josh's mouth went dry. It looked like he really might be going to jail. He tried to speak, but his voice wouldn't come out. Clio tried to help him.

"Dad, he didn't break in," she started, but Officer Jones raised his hand to make it clear he didn't want to hear anyone speak but Josh.

Josh took a deep breath and tried again. He could hear his voice shaking with the panic he felt. "I wasn't trying to break in, sir. My mom wanted me to take them some cookies and the door was open. I tried knocking but they didn't hear me. I just wanted to give them the basket of cookies." He sounded pitiful, even to himself. "And I didn't mean to take the picture. I just picked it up to look at it and …" He thought for a moment whether to tell him about Beatrice appearing, but he decided that Officer Jones was not likely to believe him and would probably think Josh was trying to be funny, which is the last thing he needed to be doing right now. "I picked it up and I heard Mr. and Mrs. Waters pull up. I just got scared and ran. I forgot I even had the picture!" This was all true enough.

Officer Jones had been staring him straight in the eyes. He must have believed that Josh was telling the truth and that it was all a misunderstanding, because he relaxed a bit. For a moment he sat there on Josh's bed looking at his hands, and then over at his daughter. Finally, he seemed to make up his mind.

"Alright, it's time I explained some things about the Waters. If I answer all of your questions, maybe you'll be able to understand why they're so on edge," he began. Clio, Josh, and Tom were all ears. "The Waters had a daughter about your age. As you apparently already know, her name was Beatrice. The family went on vacation last year to a big lake. They spent their days out on a boat, swimming and enjoying the sunshine. But on their last day there, a tragedy struck. From what I've heard, Beatrice was actually a pretty good swimmer, but sometimes the waves can be too much no matter how strong you are. They were on the lake relaxing. The area they had stopped at was supposed to be a no wake zone, but it was a busy day, I guess, and the water got rough. Beatrice was getting smacked around by the waves that had been stirred up when her life jacket broke. It took her parents a few minutes to realize something was wrong. By then Beatrice had been dragged away from them by the current and was starting to sink. They tried everything they could to save her, but she had drifted so far from the boat that by the time they got to her it was too late. She had drowned."

The three kids sat there in shock. It was one thing to think that Beatrice was a ghost. But they hadn't really thought about her dying. Beatrice was a girl their age, pretty, with blonde hair and a cute giggle. And she had died, alone and afraid, while she was supposed to be having fun, playing like any other kid. Josh was starting to understand why his parents hadn't wanted him to know. They weren't hiding secrets; they were trying to protect him.

"Of course, Mr. and Mrs. Waters were grief-stricken," Clio's dad continued with a hollow look in his eyes. He reached out and put his hand on Clio's foot. "No parent should have to go through losing a child. I don't know how they are able to keep going. They decided that it was too much for them to continue living in the house Beatrice had grown up in. So they packed everything up and moved here, where there wouldn't be as many memories haunting them. Guys," he said, looking at the three of them with real concern, "Mr. and Mrs. Waters are trying to deal with a lot of pain and grief. I know they can seem standoffish, and they may be quick to blame you for any misstep. But remember, it's probably hard for them to see happy healthy kids running around and getting into mischief.

They just want some peace and quiet to be able to move on with their lives. I need you all to promise me that you're going to leave them alone."

Josh, Tom, and Clio all looked at each other with mixture of sadness, fear, and excitement. All three felt bad for the Waters family and they didn't want to cause any trouble. But Josh could see in Tom's eyes that the story had only made him more interested in talking to Beatrice's ghost. That made Josh feel uneasy.

"Now," Officer Jones went on, "we still have to deal with the missing picture. I believe you when you say you didn't mean to take it. So all I'm going to do is make you bring it back." He got up and started toward the door. Clio's eyes looked as shocked as Josh felt. "Well," her dad said, "come on!"

CHAPTER SEVEN

Josh couldn't believe this was happening. Clio looked like any kid who was in trouble with her father—embarrassed and repentant. But to Josh this felt much more serious. He was being escorted by a police officer to go and confess to a crime. He had never really been in trouble before, and the looks he got from his parents as he was escorted by Officer Jones through the living room made his head fall in shame. Only Tom seemed unfazed by the situation. In fact, he kept trying to get Josh's attention. "Psst ... hey! Josh ... psst!"

Josh tried his best to ignore Tom's whispers. What was he thinking? He was just going to get them all in more trouble! They needed to show they were sorry and do what they were told, otherwise things could get a lot worse.

But Tom wouldn't stop. Finally, when they were outside and Officer Jones' long strides had opened up some distance between him and the kids, Josh turned to Tom and hissed, "What do you want? Can't you see how bad this is? Be quiet!"

"Josh," Tom replied, "if we give back the picture, we won't be able to see Beatrice anymore."

Josh had already thought of that. In fact it was the first thought that had gone through his head when Clio's dad said they had to take it back. But what could they do?

"So?" he snarled.

"So?" Tom stopped in his tracks.

Josh was so upset over losing the picture and losing his chance to see Beatrice again, that he didn't know what to say or do. He was angry, and he needed to direct those feelings at someone. He knew Tom was trying to be helpful, but he was there and Josh just had to let it out.

"Do you have any bright ideas to get us out of this? Some 'alien spray' that's going to keep the police away? No? Then why can't you just be quiet and do what you're told like the rest of us?"

To Josh's surprise, Tom didn't look hurt or upset. He looked angry. "I didn't know you gave up on your friends that easily," he said as he stomped by, catching up with Clio.

"Alright," Officer Jones said, turning, "that's enough talking. Josh, you're the one who took the picture, you get to do the honors and ring the doorbell."

Josh dutifully climbed the steps. He was suddenly aware of the fact that everyone on this street could see them and would know how much trouble they must be in to have a policeman escorting them. He reached out his hand and rang the bell. Then he waited. He could hear Clio's fast and frightened breathing to his left, and could see Tom's still angry red face shining to his right. It felt like they were standing on the gallows, waiting for the axe to fall.

Aaargh!

It sounded like screaming coming from the inside of the house, which was then followed by terrible crashing noises. They turned to see what Officer Jones was going to do, but he was standing at the bottom of the steps focused on his radio. Stomping footsteps came toward them and the door was jerked open by Mr. Waters, who looked distracted and disheveled. When he saw the children, his eyes became dark and he scowled so deeply that Josh thought his bushy eyebrows were going to slide over his eyes completely. Thankfully, Officer Jones spoke from the bottom of the porch steps before Mr. Waters had a chance to start yelling at them.

"How are you doing today, sir? I'm responding to the call your wife made a little while ago about these children harassing you," he said. "I've had a long talk with them and they have something to say." He gave them a stern look.

"We're sorry that we've been bothering you," Clio said, trying to sound as earnest as possible.

"I'm glad you're not an alien," Tom said, staring at Mr. Waters' shoes.

In the room behind Mr. Waters, Josh could see Beatrice standing there, looking sadder than ever. Seeing her like that broke his heart. "I am so sorry," he said, looking right at her and wanting to cry.

"Thank you for your apologies," Mr. Waters said in a rushed tone, "and thank you for your help officer." He began to close the door. Josh's heart started to beat faster. Mr. Waters hadn't waited for the picture! Now maybe he could keep it!

"Hold on!" Officer Jones called up to him. "I think Josh here has something else to say."

Mr. Waters stopped and opened the door back up. Josh looked at Clio's father pleadingly, but Officer Jones nodded toward the picture Clio had been hiding behind her back. She frowned and handed it to him. Josh looked up at Beatrice again to see her face full of surprise and confusion.

"I guess I need to give this back too," he said with a lump in his throat. "I really didn't mean to take it."

Mr. Waters' eyes got big as he looked at the gold framed photo in Josh's hand.

"We'll miss seeing Beatrice!" Tom blurted out. Mr. Waters stared at him, looking shocked.

As soon as Tom said it, Mrs. Waters came flying from the next room, bumping into furniture as she raced to the door.

Josh felt all the blood drain from his face as she lunged toward him, snatching the picture away, and slammed the door.

* * *

The next day at school the three of them sat moping at the lunch table. Clio had her arms crossed in front of her, staring off in the distance, while Tom had his head propped up on his hand, playing with the peas on his plate.

"I can't believe your parents called mine afterwards," Tom complained to Josh. "Now I'm grounded for two whole weeks! What am I supposed to do without my phone? I'm going to be so behind on my videos!"

"You think that's bad?" Clio whined, "my dad won't let me watch any TV for like a month. I'm going to miss all of my shows."

Josh sighed sadly. Was this all his fault? His friends were being punished for something that he had dragged them into. They should have had nothing to do with any of it, and here they all were, grounded from all of their favorite things. He was grounded too, but he cared less about his phone and electronics, and more about the fact that he would never be able to see Beatrice again. Things would go back to normal, but they would never be the same for Josh. After all of this, he had become friends with a ghost, and now he had to go on pretending that he'd never even known her. He didn't even have the picture to prove that she was real. All he had left of her was the memory.

"What do you think will happen to Beatrice?" he asked.

"I've actually been thinking a lot about that," Clio said. "You know, after you took the picture, her parents must not have been able to see her anymore."

"Yeah, she told me that she thought they were ignoring her," Josh replied. He was starting to see what Clio was getting at and it made him feel even worse.

"Well, maybe it's a good thing that we had to give it back to them then. Can you imagine living in a house with your family, but no one can see you? How lonely must that have been for her."

"She wasn't 'living' there," Tom grumbled into his peas. "A ghost can't be 'living' somewhere." He was still mad that Josh hadn't done something to stop Officer Jones from making them give it back.

What was I supposed to do, Josh thought, *grab his handcuffs and cuff him?* He had done what he had to do, that's all there was to it. And maybe Clio was right. Maybe keeping the picture was making things worse for Beatrice and it was actually a good thing that her parents had it back now.

"I do worry about her mom, though," Clio said thoughtfully. "That woman seems off."

"Yeah, Beatrice even said that she could get really mad sometimes," Josh remembered.

"And what had all that noise been about?" Clio asked.

"It sounded like she was ripping up the house and having a mental breakdown," Josh said. "And with the way Mr. Waters was acting, it makes a lot of sense."

"After everything they've been through ... the poor family," Clio said sympathetically.

"Well it's none of our business anymore," Josh finally decided. They were already in enough trouble. There was nothing they could do—it would be better to just move on and forget anything had happened.

"I disagree," Tom said gravely. "I don't think this is over yet."

CHAPTER EIGHT

The next few days went by pretty miserably for the trio. Being grounded was no fun at all because there was nothing to do. Josh, Tom, and Clio all spent their weekends alone in their rooms with no phones, no TV, nothing. There wasn't anything to do except try to pretend that everything was normal and okay again, even though it wasn't.

Going back to school Monday morning actually didn't sound so bad. Then they would be able to see each other again and have something to do, at least for a little while. When Josh was grounded, one of the rules was not having any friends over. The trio still had to get their history project done though, so Josh's parents made a compromise and were allowing Josh's friends to come over after school on the last day of the week.

Josh couldn't wait for the next Friday to come, when he didn't have to get off the school bus by himself. He had started to feel like he was being watched, and it was freaking him out. Mr. Waters had never seemed interested in spending time outside until after the day that Officer Jones had made them take the picture back. Now it was as if Mr. Waters always had an excuse to be outside when Josh came walking by their house to get to his own.

On Monday, Mr. Waters was mowing the grass.

On Tuesday, he sat outside with a book.

On Wednesday, he was cleaning the car.

On Thursday, he was on the phone.

And every single day that he was outside and Josh walked by, it took everything Josh had in him to not run away screaming. Most neighbors would do the friendly, neighborly thing, and wave or say hello as Josh passed by. But not Mr. Waters. He never looked happy. Mr. Waters wore a frown so deep that Josh wondered if he would need to have surgery to ever be able to smile again. Whenever Josh would pass by his house, he swore he could feel Mr. Waters' eyes on him. But whenever he would try to look back at him, Mr. Waters would avert his eyes, pretending to be busy with whatever he was doing that day. The few times that their eyes did meet, Mr. Waters' intense stare sent chills down Josh's spine, making him uneasy and wanting more than ever to get inside as quickly as possible.

To make matters even more suspicious, Mr. Waters almost always went back inside once Josh was inside too. Josh knew this because he would sometimes check from the window. It was as if he was being watched by Mr. Waters.

He didn't want to tell his friends at first, afraid that he might come off as being paranoid. But after almost a full week of it, he couldn't hold it in anymore. That Friday at the lunch table, he decided to share his concerns.

"Guys," Josh began as he sat down at last with his tray, "I think Mr. Waters is stalking me."

Josh expected Clio's facial expression to begin to scrunch into one that would say, "That's ridiculous, why would you think such a stupid thing?" but it didn't. Instead, she looked concerned and said, "Why do you think that, Josh?"

"He has been outside every single day this week when I get off the bus," he explained.

"I bet he and that old witch Mrs. Waters are up to something," Tom offered. "You never can trust a witch."

At this point, Josh didn't know what to think. "You guys are riding the bus with me to my house to work on the project tonight, right?"

Tom and Clio both confirmed that they were. "Good. I don't know if I can handle walking by his house alone again, feeling like he's out to get me."

But that afternoon when they got off the bus, Mr. Waters was nowhere to be seen. "I could have sworn that he would be out here," Josh half whispered to Tom and Clio as they walked past the Waters house.

"Look, the car is gone," Clio pointed out.

"That's so weird," Josh said, "he's been out there every day this week and it's been creeping me out."

"I don't know. But I don't think hanging around here for very long is such a good idea," Clio said. They had stopped in their tracks without realizing it, and now they were looking up at the Waters house. "We have a project that we need to work on. Come on Tom," Clio motioned. "Tom?"

Josh and Clio both turned around to find that he wasn't behind them like they'd thought. Looking around quickly, they spotted him inching his way closer to the house.

"Tom!" Clio yelled, but he wasn't listening. "Tom!" She yelled again, this time taking off toward him to drag him back. Not knowing what else to do, Josh followed her.

"What do you think you're doing?" Clio screamed at Tom, "You're going to get us in so much trouble!" Josh was looking around frantically to make sure no one saw what was going on.

"I just wanted to check something," Tom said.

Just then, Josh heard a noise not that far off. "Clio …" he spoke uneasily.

"Seriously Tom, I don't want to get grounded for even longer!" She was still carrying on.

"Clio!" Josh finally got her attention. "Do you guys hear that?" The trio was silent for a moment.

"It sounds like footsteps. Someone's coming from behind the house! Hide!" Clio whispered, and the three of them dove into the nearest bushes.

They sat in complete silence, listening to the footsteps. The steps got closer and closer until it seemed like whoever it was, was right on top of them. All three held their breaths, not daring to make any noise for a long time. Minutes passed, and they began to doubt that it had been anything at all.

"Do you think they're gone?" Tom whispered.

Josh was just about to peek out when—

"YOWWW" Tom yelled as he was yanked straight off of the ground and out of the bushes.

Clio squeaked in fear and Josh gasped in shock.

"It's time for the games to stop. Come on out," came a familiar voice.

Trembling and left with no other options, Josh and Clio stood up slowly, trying their best not to scratch themselves on the branches. Standing in front of them was the angry face that Josh had become all too familiar with in the past week. Mr. Waters had caught them once again.

"We didn't mean to cause any more problems Mr. Waters," Clio begged.

"Yeah, we were just leaving," Josh said.

"You're not going anywhere," Mr. Waters rumbled. The trio all exchanged scared glances. "We need to talk."

CHAPTER NINE

"I need your help," Mr. Waters began.

Our help? Josh thought. This was definitely not what he had expected at all.

"I know that there are rumors going around about us. In fact, I started most of them. But it's time that you kids found out the truth," Mr. Waters said. This really seemed like it was something serious.

"We're sorry for your loss," Clio said.

"Yeah, we know she drowned while you were on vacation," Tom said triumphantly.

"And we know about her ghost and the picture!" Josh's eyes got big and his face flushed with embarrassment and fear.

Mr. Waters stared at him for a moment. "Well, she didn't just drown, and we weren't on vacation." He looked down for a moment.

"What happened to her, Mr. Waters?" Clio asked, looking sympathetic.

"We had taken a trip to teach Beatrice about nymphs—" he began to explain.

"Oh! I know what those are!" Tom interrupted. "They're a type of water spirit!"

"That's correct," Mr. Waters looked both surprised and impressed by Tom's knowledge. "I can teach you more about them later if you're interested." Tom looked *very interested.* "Now as I was saying," he continued, "we were teaching Beatrice how to handle and communicate with nymphs—"

"Wait, hold on," Clio interrupted. She had come to terms with the idea that ghosts were real, but she wasn't quite ready to just accept casual conversations about water spirits. "What are you talking about? Nymphs?"

"Ah, yes, I should have said. You see, Mrs. Waters and I are magicians. Not the type who shoot sparks out of a wand or pull rabbits out of hats, like you might read about in your books. Real magicians. We study ancient teachings to learn to communicate with spirits and gain some control over the natural world."

Josh stood there with his mouth open. He had thought there was nothing else that could surprise him, but he was wrong.

"We were raising Beatrice to follow in our footsteps and that's why she was out on the water—to learn to talk to the nymphs. She really was a great swimmer, and even if she hadn't been, the nymphs would've helped her. She was doing well with it all. So well in fact, that Lisa, Mrs. Waters, thought she could do something a little more challenging. Most nymphs are friendly and playful creatures, but you have to be careful choosing which ones you want to play with. Some just don't understand that we aren't as strong as them, or that we can't breathe underwater like they do. We had summoned a nymph that we were familiar with, and Beatrice had really gotten the hang of communicating with it. It was going great, so Lisa decided Beatrice needed something more challenging, but I disagreed. So when I walked to the other side of the boat to get a soda, she summoned a different nymph for Beatrice—one that was much more difficult to handle. By the time I got back, Beatrice was struggling in the water. Her life jacket wasn't enough to save her from a childish nymph that was determined to bring her new friend under the lake with her. Lisa had already jumped into the water and was trying to swim to her rescue, but she couldn't reach her fast enough before she was pulled under. The entire time, I was trying everything I knew to try to save her. I tried banishing, protection spells, and even throwing things at the nymph, but none of it worked. There was nothing we could do. All that was left was the life jacket that bubbled back up to the surface." He paused for a moment, looking sadder and more regretful than Josh had ever seen anyone be. He must have felt absolutely horrible.

"That's awful," Josh said.

"You have to understand how much Lisa and I loved Beatrice. She was our world. We simply couldn't go on without her. After doing some research, her mother discovered a way we wouldn't have to. It is an ancient spell that links a spirit to an object. Maybe you've heard the stories of genies and their lamps. That is essentially the same type of magic. We worked hard to arrange things just right for this complicated ritual. Finally, we were able to bind her spirit to the picture so that she could always be with us. We thought our family could be happy forever." He trailed off and slumped as he thought about the situation.

"That changed," he went on, "when you showed up, Josh Martin."

Josh looked at the other two. They seemed just as amazed and confused as he felt. Even Tom, who believed every crazy story he ever heard, looked shocked and moved by the story.

"How did he change that, Mr. Waters?" Clio asked.

"Josh, why did you take the picture?" Mr. Waters asked him.

"I really didn't mean to!" he exclaimed. "I was trying to bring over a house warming present and I just saw the picture lying there." He wasn't sure whether he should say the next part, but at this point he figured the truth was important, even if it was embarrassing. "I thought she looked pretty," he said, blushing from the top of his head down to his toes. "So I picked it up. And then she was really there. I thought she must have been hiding behind one of the boxes. She seemed really happy to have another kid her age to talk to. She said she was lonely and so we spent time talking. She thought you'd be mad if you found out she'd been there alone with me, so when you came home she told me to run. I forgot I still had the picture until I was outside. By then I didn't know how to return it without making you even madder."

"Mmm," Mr. Waters seemed to genuinely understand. "Well, when you left with the picture, her mother and I could no longer see or hear her. It was like we'd lost her all over again. Lisa couldn't handle it. She started going crazy from the grief. She has always been more willing to dabble in the, er, darker sides of magic. When you took the picture, she was ready to do some very nasty things. I was able to convince her not to hurt you, in case she accidentally did something to harm Beatrice as well. But you were not safe."

Mr. Waters just told Josh that he had protected him, maybe even saved him from Mrs. Waters. But for some reason that didn't make him feel any better. And knowing he could do magic sure didn't make Mr. Waters any less scary.

"Let me ask you," Mr. Waters continued, "how did you figure out what the picture was?"

"That was me!" Tom exclaimed.

Mr. Waters looked at him again. "Yes, I can imagine it was. You are very perceptive."

Tom beamed. "So now we come to the part I need your help with. When you brought the picture back, we thought our family could be whole again. But it wasn't. You see, Beatrice had not known she was dead. When her mother and I couldn't see her, we didn't realize she was still in the house with us. Honestly, we assumed that her spirit had gone with the picture. As I said, this is an old and difficult type of magic, and not many people have done it successfully, so we weren't exactly sure. As it turns out, she stayed with us in the house. At first she thought that we were angry and ignoring her. But then she heard us talking and realized that she was, as you put it, a ghost. She was scared and heartbroken. And she was very alone. After we got the picture back, she was able to tell us how much you meant to her, Josh. I know you only got to speak to her a few times, but to a young girl who has lost her friends and has no one else to talk to, it meant the world."

Josh's heart swelled with joy when he heard this, and he could feel his face blushing again.

"One thing she has made clear," Mr. Waters went on, "is that she is not happy here. She is caught between two worlds. She has her mother and me, but she can't go out and do the things a girl her age should do. She can't go to school, or make friends, or play. She can't grow up. As she put it, she simply exists. She wants us to let her go so she can move on."

Josh, Clio, and Tom all looked at him with sadness and disbelief in their eyes. They had never even considered what Beatrice must be feeling to be trapped as a ghost like she was. Josh felt especially guilty, because all he had been worried about were his own feelings about her.

"So are you going to release her from the picture?" Clio asked.

"Well, it's more complicated than that. You see, in order to release her, the picture has to be destroyed while Beatrice's hand is touching it," he explained.

"If she wants to move on, that shouldn't be a problem," Tom said.

"The issue isn't Beatrice," Mr. Waters' eyes get dark and his face became hard. "The problem is Mrs. Waters. She won't listen. Ever since Beatrice's death, Mrs. Waters has been losing her grip. I'm afraid she's going insane. When Beatrice told her that she wanted to be released, her mother became enraged. She became violent. When she realized she couldn't intimidate Beatrice or me into backing down, she went further. She trapped Beatrice in a magical triangle. Once inside, no spirit is able to escape unless they are allowed out. Beatrice was already alone and miserable, now she is imprisoned by her own mother."

Clio and Josh looked terrified at what they'd just heard, but Tom just looked angry.

"Why are you telling us all this?" Tom asked Mr. Waters.

"I'm going to free her," he said, "but I need your help."

CHAPTER TEN
BEATRICE

Beatrice was afraid. "There's no reason to be scared," Mrs. Waters was trying to soothe her. "This is just for your protection. Once I'm sure you're safe you'll be free to run around like you've always done."

Beatrice was huddled into a ball on the floor. Around her was a magical triangle with foreign cursive-looking writing on it. A blue light rose up from it around her. When she was first trapped inside it, Beatrice had tried to walk out. As soon as she touched the blue light it had felt like she was being shocked, burned, and frozen all at the same time. Now she was scared to move at all because she didn't want to accidentally touch it again.

"Come on, Beatrice. I hate seeing you just lying there that way," her mom seemed both frustrated and sad.

Tears welled up in Beatrice's eyes. "I shouldn't be here," she said, her emotions making her words come out as a whisper. "I don't belong here."

She had known something wasn't right for some time, but it wasn't until she heard her parents talking that she found out about her death. At first she couldn't believe it, but then memories started flooding back. She remembered being pulled down into the water by the nymphs. She could feel the horrible burning in her lungs when she tried to hold her breath, fighting to swim back to the surface. Then the flood of clear fluid filling her chest as she slipped away into the bright light of the afterlife. And, oh, what peace she had felt while she was there. She remembered the feeling of comfort, floating in the light. There were countless others around her floating in it too, and they were all so peaceful and happy. But then she felt something else. At first it was a tug, like a gentle current in the lake. But the tug became a tear and she felt like she was being ripped in half. The light disappeared and she was covered in pain and darkness. For a long time now, she had felt scared and out of place in her old surroundings. Now she knew why and she yearned to go back to the afterlife where she belonged.

"Please," she pleaded in a small voice. "You have to let me go. I don't belong here anymore."

"Yes you do, Beatrice! You were never meant to die! You should have never died!"

"But I did, Mom. And now I need to be able to move on."

"No," her mother's eyes were filling with tears. "I can't let you go again, Beatrice. I didn't deserve to lose you."

"I'm not happy here. I can't spend eternity trapped in this closet! You've got to let me go!" Beatrice was frantic.

"But we can be happy together here! We can talk and spend time together—like we used to!"

"How can you think this is okay? You've got me locked up. I'm not your daughter, I'm your prisoner!"

"I'm trying to save your life, and you want to leave me forever?" her mother shrieked.

Desperate, Beatrice threw herself against the barrier of the magic triangle. Each time she bounced back with a pop that sounded like a bone snapping.

"Stop that!" her mother said rolling her eyes. "There's no way for you to break out of that triangle. I'll let you out once I'm sure that you are safe and—" Mrs. Waters lost sight of her daughter.

"Beatrice? Beatrice! Where did you go?" Mrs. Waters suddenly yelled. Beatrice looked up, giving her mom a confused look. She hadn't moved and was still right where she'd fallen from her last attempt to break out. How could she not see her?

Mrs. Waters ran to the window. "No!" she screamed. Beatrice watched as her mom took off down the stairs. "John!" she heard her yelling, "Bring that picture back!"

Beatrice heard the front door slam, leaving her completely alone and scared, trapped in a triangle in a dark closet.

CHAPTER ELEVEN

Josh, Tom, and Clio crouched behind the tree in Josh's front yard. "Is she gone yet?" Clio asked. They were waiting for Mrs. Waters to leave the house.

"Not yet," Josh replied, peeking out from behind the tree. He glanced down at the picture of Beatrice in his hand, hoping that the plan would work. Mr. Waters had given them Beatrice's picture and told them to hide behind the tree at Josh's house, then he had run off in the other direction.

The idea was that, when Josh took the picture away from the Waters' house, Beatrice would disappear and Mrs. Waters would go after her husband, thinking he had taken it. That would give them time to get into the house and find the magical tools they needed to free Beatrice. Mr. Waters explained that they had to find the spell book to free her from the triangle, and the magic hammer to destroy the picture. To break the spell binding her, Beatrice would have to be touching the picture when the hammer was used to destroy it. Mr. Waters made it all sound like he was giving instructions on something simple like baking cookies, but to Josh it all sounded insane. And with his luck lately, he worried that something would go wrong. What if Mrs. Waters wasn't with Beatrice when she disappeared? What if they couldn't find the magical items? What if she caught them all red handed? It was almost too much for him to bear. His heart was pounding as the seconds ticked by.

"There she goes!" Tom exclaimed as he watched Mrs. Waters hop into her car and drive off. Tom was bouncing and ready to go.

"Shh, don't yell!" Clio hissed, clasping her hand over Tom's mouth. "We have to wait until she's far enough away." The group huddled around, their bodies tense as they waited for the right moment.

"Okay, now!" Josh whispered. They crawled as fast as they could back over to Beatrice's house. Josh hoped no one saw them. He knew they must have looked really silly, but they were so afraid of Mrs. Waters that they were scared to stand up and run in case she got suspicious and looked back. By the time they got to the house, Josh's hands and knees felt like he'd fallen off his bike down a gravel mountain.

Standing on the porch, they looked at each other. Josh saw the fear in his friends' eyes and realized how much danger they were in. He couldn't help but feel like this was all his fault. If anything happened to them, he didn't think he could live with himself.

"This is your last chance to back out," Josh told them. "Once we go through this door it's too late. I don't know what might happen, but I've got to help Beatrice. I won't blame either of you if you don't want to go through with this."

Tom and Clio looked at him with a strange look. Why did he say all of that? Now they were going to leave and he was going to be alone. He felt sick with fear.

Clio's face turned hard. "Shut up, Josh!" she said. "We're not leaving you and we're not leaving Beatrice!" It took a second for Josh to register what she had said. Slowly a smile spread across her face and she put her hand on his shoulder.

"Alright!" Josh smiled, the nerves starting to turn into excitement. "Let's do this!"

They burst into the house in such a hurry that they nearly forgot to shut the door behind them. "Come on, we have to find Beatrice!" Josh exclaimed, leading the group up the stairs.

"Beatrice!" they all started yelling, poking their heads in each room that they passed.

"Josh?" He heard a small voice coming from one of the rooms. Wherever she was, she sounded really scared.

"Beatrice!" He yelled again, hoping to follow the direction of her voice.

"Josh!" She yelled back. They found where they thought her voice was coming from, but the door to the room was locked.

"What do we do?" Josh gasped in panic. He looked over to Clio, who looked as confused and scared as he felt. "Please tell me you have some idea," he said to her.

Clio just looked at him with big eyes and shook her head. Josh felt like he wanted to cry.

"Uh, guys," Tom said from behind them. Josh turned to see Tom standing there with a goofy grin on his face. "You know, I've watched videos online about picking locks. Step aside," he said. He took a paper clip out of his pocket and went to work. Josh was speechless as he heard a few clicks in the lock and then saw the door swing open. "After you," Tom said with a very proud look on his face.

Josh actually smiled for a second as he stepped past his friend and into the room. That smile disappeared as he looked around and saw that Beatrice was nowhere to be seen. Instead, there was a strange room filled with all sorts of oddities--big black and white pillars, altars in every corner, weird signs that seemed to have different languages and strange symbols on them. Josh had never seen anything like it. He realized that many of the things he'd seen in the box with Beatrice's picture that first day were scattered around the room. He looked everywhere, searching for a sign of where Beatrice could be.

"The closet!" Clio pointed. Josh had nearly missed it because of the giant banner hanging from the handle. They rushed over, flinging the door open. There, in a cocoon of blue light, stood Beatrice.

Josh was so excited to see her again that he reached out to hug her. But when his arms and body hit the blue light bordering the triangle, they bounced back like an energy was pushing them. Beatrice gave him a sad look in response to his confused one.

He looked down. So this was what Mr. Waters was talking about. Josh had no idea how a triangle could hold a ghost in and a living body out, but that didn't matter right now. All that mattered was following Mr. Waters' instructions so they could save Beatrice!

"I'm gonna get you out of here," he promised her. He turned to Clio and Tom. "Her dad said there's a book around here with spells that will help us release her from the triangle.

We've got to find it. Fast!" The closet was pretty spacious and it didn't look much different than the outside room.

"Look inside the chest there. I think she shoved it in there before she ran away," Beatrice spoke. The three gathered around to open the chest. It was oddly quiet as they all held their breaths and lifted the lid. There lying on top of what appeared to be a bunch of different colored robes and funny hats was a thick leather-bound book. Together, they set it on top of the chest and opened it up.

Josh's fingers were tingling. He wasn't sure if it was from the excitement and nervousness, or maybe from the magical power that this book held. There was so much information in it. How were they ever going to be able to find the right spell?

"While you guys try to find the spell, I'm going to go look for the magic hammer that Mr. Waters said we need to use on the picture. I think he said he kept it in the dresser of his nightstand," Clio said. Then she ran out the room to go search.

Finding the right spell seemed hopeless to Josh and Tom. There was just too much to go through, and most of it wasn't even written in English! It would have been so much easier if Mr. Waters had told them what the name of the spell was, or what page it was on.

They were passing a page with a picture of what looked like a frog with a human head when they heard a noise and stopped their page-flipping.

"Did you hear that?" Tom whispered. His face had turned as pale as a ghost—paler than Beatrice's. "I think she's back!" In a panic, Tom grabbed the book and jumped behind a large statue of a dog-headed man with a flower in his hand at the back of the closet.

Josh looked around frantically for another place to hide. He darted out of the closet and dove under one of the altars, pulling the colorful cloth over the side to hide him. The table cloth was long enough to completely cover him, and he was sure he wouldn't be found there. As he sat there clinging to Beatrice's picture and shaking, he wondered where Clio had ended up, and if she was okay. *Why did I drag my best friends into this?*

CHAPTER TWELVE
CLIO

Clio found the magic hammer in Mr. Waters' night stand, right where he said it was. It didn't look like any hammer she'd ever seen before. The top of the hammer was big and square, with both sides flat and identical. The handle and top were made from one piece of a shining blue stone, and it had silver writing all over it in some language she'd never seen before. As she looked at it, she couldn't tell if it was shining because of how it reflected the light or if it was glowing from some power of its own.

I hope the boys have found the book. I better get back quick; they're probably going to need my help to find the right spell. Clio turned to rush back down to the strange magical room. She was jumping down the stairs two at a time when the front door flew open. Mrs. Waters barged in through the doorway, leaving Clio no time to hide. She was standing right there in front of Mrs. Waters, frozen in fear and unable to do anything except look at her with wide, frightened eyes.

"You!" Mrs. Waters yelled. Clio was shocked to see that she looked terrified too. Clio had no time to respond before Mrs. Waters started muttering strange words. She lifted up her hand and a bolt of red lightning came flying toward Clio. She didn't have time to think. Panicking, Clio lifted her arms in front of her to protect her face. *I'm dead!* She thought, closing her eyes.

BANG! THUMP!

Clio felt like she'd just been hit by a bus, but she was still standing and she didn't feel dead. Slowly, she opened her eyes and was shocked to see Mrs. Waters laying on the floor, several feet from where she had been standing only moments before. Clio looked down at the hammer in her hand. It wasn't just shining anymore; it was lit up like a light bulb with brilliant blue light.

Mrs. Waters stumbled back to her feet with pure hatred on her face. As she started to mutter another spell, Clio had an idea. Maybe it was the hammer that had saved her! Just then a ball of green came hurtling toward Clio. She didn't duck or try to jump out of the way. She raised the hammer and swung it like a baseball bat.

The vibrant green ball bounced off of it and hit a big clock that was against the wall beside Mrs. Waters. It came crashing down and the angry old woman had to jump out of the way. Clio didn't hesitate. She leapt down the rest of the stairs and ran down the hall to the room where the Beatrice was.

Clio burst through the door and felt her stomach drop when she saw it was empty. "Guys? Where are you?" she asked in a strangled voice. She could hear Mrs. Waters' footsteps marching down the hall.

"Under here, quick!" Josh cried, grabbing her ankle.

"AHHHHHHH!" Clio screamed, clamping her hand over her mouth.

"Now!" Josh hissed, pulling her down under the altar with him just as the door opened.

Clio held her breath as Mrs. Waters walked in. At first she seemed to be looking around, trying to find them. But once she looked inside the closet that Beatrice was in, she completely changed. She ran straight to the triangle. "Oh, there you are, Beatrice!" Mrs. Waters sounded relieved.

"Let me go! Please!" Beatrice shouted.

"I can't do that, Beatrice. You know that." Her mom was firm.

Clio and Josh stared at each other under the altar, the red cloth cover giving the light a dangerous blood-like color. "I'm going to look," Clio whispered. Josh glared at her like she was crazy, but he didn't say anything. Slowly, she peaked out the side of the altar and looked into the closet. Mrs. Waters was standing between her and the triangle. Beatrice was still trapped in the blue light, kneeling on the floor pleading with her mother. It broke Clio's heart. She was trying to figure out what to do next when she saw Tom inching around the statue in the back of the closet. He stopped and took a deep breath. With his knuckles white from holding the big leather book so tight, he jumped out and yelled at Mrs. Waters.

* TOM *

"You're not going to hurt her anymore! Electro Magnum!" he shouted. He had expected to blast her with a giant ball of electricity that would throw her across the room. Instead, he watched in horror as Mrs. Waters' hair drifted straight up in the air, standing on end from static electricity. He gulped as she turned toward him and tried to pat her hair down, but it did no good.

"I see you found my book," she said with an icy voice. "You need to gi—"

"Corpus Auto!" Tom shouted before she could finish. He hoped this would make her get run over by a car. Instead, she began to dance uncontrollably.

"Stop this nonsense this instant!" she shrieked while dancing into the bigger room, looking for a way to stop.

* CLIO *

Josh looked at Clio. "This is our chance," he whispered, "We can knock her over and lock ourselves in the closet with Beatrice."

Clio set her jaw and nodded. This was it.

They jumped out from under the altar and launched themselves at Mrs. Waters, who was still dancing uncontrollably around the room. Clio grabbed her legs and hit the ground hard when Mrs. Waters spun out of the way. Josh had better luck and tackled her to the ground, but before he could get up and run for the closet, Mrs. Waters had knocked over another altar with a wand on it. The impact stopped the spell that was making her dance. She grabbed the wand and started yelling spells at them.

"You kids have destroyed everything! I'm not letting you hurt my family anymore!" she shouted. Sparks of bright lights went flying all across the room.

Josh and Clio darted around, ducking behind furniture and objects to avoid being hit by the dangerous spells. Clio pulled the glowing hammer back out to protect herself. She gestured to Josh to run for the closet.

* JOSH *

As he turned toward Beatrice, he pulled her picture out of his pocket. *If we can just get in there and lock the door, we'll be able to release her!* He was frantic and really hoped Tom had found the right spell to break the triangle barrier.

"Wait!" Mrs. Waters yelled. "Is that—" she knocked over a pillar, "Is that *the picture*?" she immediately stopped firing spells, obviously afraid of damaging the picture.

Josh saw this as the perfect opportunity to gain the upper hand. "That's right! And if you break this," he said, holding the picture up, "Beatrice will never be yours again!" Mrs. Waters winced at his words.

Her next words were strained but calm, like a policeman trying to free hostages. "Listen to me," she said. "If that pictures breaks, Beatrice will be lost."

"We know!" Josh yelled, holding it up high above his head, threatening to smash it. "Your husband told us everything! He told us Beatrice doesn't want to be trapped here anymore. She wants to be able to move on, but you're too selfish to let her go!"

"No! You don't understand!" Mrs. Waters was pleading. "You have to have realized that Beatrice can only be seen when that picture is nearby. Breaking it like this won't free her spirit! It will just make her invisible for all of eternity! No one will be able to see or speak to her again!"

"NO!" Beatrice exclaimed and started to weep.

"You're lying!" Josh said, fear rising inside of him.

"I don't think she is, Josh," Clio whispered. "Remember, Mr. Waters said it had to be done with the hammer, while Beatrice is touching the picture. That's how we free her. But if the picture breaks, she'll just be trapped—not able to be with us here, and not able to move on."

Josh looked at Beatrice, who was gasping and shaking on the floor of the triangle in fear. Then he looked at Mrs. Waters. For the first time she seemed frail and weak. It was hard to believe that this was the same woman who was casting spells at them and who had trapped Beatrice. He almost felt sorry for her. Maybe there was a way to talk this out. Maybe now she'd be willing to listen and let Beatrice decide for herself.

As he stood there trying to figure out what to do next, Josh's hair stood on end as he heard Tom's voice starting to chant in some strange language. He turned and saw him, hand held out toward the triangle. He hoped that he found the right spell was trying to break the spell that had Beatrice trapped. This whole nightmare needed to be over. He was almost ready to smile when he heard a second voice starting to chant.

Josh could feel the picture start pulling itself from his hands. He tried grabbing it harder, but it was like his fingers were made of rubber. The picture floated up, up, up until finally, Josh couldn't hold onto it anymore.

"Yes! It's mine! Come to me!" Mrs. Waters exclaimed.

The picture hung in midair between Josh and Mrs. Waters.

CHAPTER THIRTEEN

"Stop!" someone shouted from the doorway. It was Beatrice's dad! Mrs. Waters turned with surprise, dropping her focus on the picture. Josh saw it begin to fall as if it were in slow motion.

"No!" he shouted, diving for the picture. But as his side hit the floor hard, he knew he was too far away. He cried out as he saw it coming down on its corner and hit the ground. In panic he turned to try and get one last look at Beatrice before she disappeared. But she never did. Instead, he saw her standing in her triangle with a look of desperate concentration while she was chanting under her breath. He looked back at the picture and saw that it was still standing up on its corner, gently spinning in place.

"Nice save!" Tom exclaimed from the closet. "I didn't know you could do that!"

The picture flattened gently onto the floor as Beatrice stood shaking. "I didn't know I could either. Before I died, I was learning a lot of spells. I wasn't sure if they would work now or not."

"I'd say they work great!" Tom beamed at her.

Mrs. Waters stood for a moment in shock before realizing what was happening. A look of pride in her daughter's magic crossed her face, but she didn't let herself enjoy it. She dove for the picture.

"No, Lisa." Mr. Waters said firmly as he stepped in front of her.

"You betrayed me!" Mrs. Waters screamed at her husband, clawing at his arms to try and get past him.

"This has gone too far, Lisa. It has to stop," he said with a calm voice.

It was like he had poked a bear. Mrs. Waters turned on him, flailing against him. "This is all your fault! You did this! You let her drown, you're the reason I couldn't save her. You caused all of this, you heartless monster! You're the reason the world is such an awful place!" she shrieked.

Mrs. Waters continued to scream and accuse him for quite some time. Much of what she said didn't make any sense at all. She was having a complete mental breakdown. Mr. Waters stood there and took it, continually apologizing and trying to calm her down. Josh even felt sorry for him. How long had he had to deal with someone who acted like this? He just couldn't believe it.

While Mrs. Waters was attacking him, Mr. Waters had slowly been turning so that her back was to Beatrice now. He gave the kids a side glance that seemed to say, "The book! Hurry!" Josh and Clio took the cue and quietly backed into the closet with Tom and Beatrice.

Clio closed the door slowly, trying not to bring any attention to them, then she grabbed some of the weird magical stuff around the closet and piled it, blocking the door for good measure. "There, that ought to do it," she said, brushing her hands off. "Have you found the spell yet?"

"No," Tom said with a frustrated sigh.

"Here, let me see it," said Clio, snatching the book.

"Hey! I can find it myself!" Tom argued, trying to get the book back.

"Be careful!" Josh said, just as a sickening *rip* tore the air.

"Look what you did!" Clio shouted.

"Me? You're the one trying to steal it!" Tom cried defensively.

Josh grabbed the book, but as he took it, a pile of papers fell out of it.

"Look!" Beatrice exclaimed, "there was a pocket in the back of it! What are all those papers?"

Josh and Tom started laying the papers out on the floor for Beatrice to see while Clio started looking more closely at the book. While they looked at the pages, Josh began to get chills. All of the papers in that pocket had been about Beatrice. There were ones about bringing a spirit back from the dead, and about locking one in a triangle, but he had expected to see that. What made him feel a quiet terror rising inside him were the other ones. Folded together was a stack that had Beatrice's name written on them. Inside there were instructions on how to raise a dark demon to kill anyone you wanted—and Josh felt his stomach turn when he saw his name on the page, along with Tom's and Clio's. As scary as that was, it was nothing compared to the next page. On it were instructions on how to bind a spirit to a dead body to bring them back to life. Scrawled across the top was Clio's name in blood red ink. Josh could only stare in horror.

"What's wrong?" Beatrice asked him. He looked up and could see the confusion on her face.

"It's nothing," Josh tried to lie, but his hands were shaking.

"Tell me," she said.

"She wouldn't ..." Tom was looking over Josh's shoulder.

"What?" Beatrice demanded, looking as pale as a ghost.

"You're mom isn't finished," Josh finally said.

"What do you mean?"

"She doesn't just want you to stay with her as a spirit. She has a plan to give you a new body."

"How could she do that?" Beatrice asked. "She can't just make a new one for me. Magic doesn't work that way."

"No," he said. "She isn't going to make one, she's going to take one."

Clio had put the book aside and walked over to Josh. When she saw the papers, her eyes became wide with horror. "She's going to kill us!" she screamed. "She's going to kill all of us and then give you my body!"

"OK, we can't panic," Beatrice said with a strength that seemed bigger than her small body could hold. "We can stop this. You just have to break the picture."

"We know!" Clio snapped. "But how do we do that without the spell to break the triangle?"

"That's not what I meant," Beatrice said. "Now that we know what she is planning on doing, we can't risk waiting. She could come through that door any second. You can't wait to free me. Just break it now."

Josh's heart sank. "Beatrice, we can't do that! You'd be trapped forever! You'd never be able to cross into the afterlife and no one alive would be able to see you!"

"I know," she said quietly. "But it's the only way. I won't let her hurt you like she's hurt me."

Just then, they heard the door starting to shake.

"She's right," Clio said in an emotionless voice. "I'm not going to die for this."

"No!" Josh shouted; he couldn't believe what he was hearing. "I'm not going to give up on you, Beatrice!"

"You have to, it's the only way to save yourself," she reassured him. "I can't spend the rest of eternity knowing that you were hurt because of me."

The door rattled louder as Mrs. Waters tried to break in. Clio picked up the glowing hammer.

"I'm sorry, Beatrice," she said. "You are a really nice girl. I wish we could have gotten to know each other better." She walked over to the picture that was laying on the floor.

"Stop!" Josh yelled, trying to grab the picture too, but he was too far away.

"I'm sorry, Josh," Clio said as she began to lift the hammer. But just as Josh could feel the panic rising inside him, Tom grabbed Clio's arms.

"We can't do this," he said, huffing and puffing as Clio struggled against him.

"You have to!" Beatrice yelled, as the door began to give way and they could see light starting to pour in through a crack in it.

Josh picked up the picture and ran over to Beatrice. "I can't let you do this," he said to her.

"It's okay, Josh," she said, looking him straight in the eye. "I'll be fine."

The door finally burst open just as Clio was able to push Tom away. She raised the hammer high above her head and ran over swinging it down toward the picture.

"NO!" Mrs. Waters shrieked, *"SPIRITUS LIBERATE!"*

There was a popping sound and a flash of orange light. Josh looked up and saw the hammer coming down as Beatrice stepped out of the triangle. For one split second, for the very first time, he felt her hand touch his as she laid her hand on the picture. She was freezing cold at first. Then he felt the crushing blow of the hammer and the picture shatter into thousands of shards of glittering glass. Josh was sure that her hand seemed to suddenly solidify and heat up in that very moment. He looked up and saw Beatrice's smiling blue eyes starting to fade from sight as the warmth of her hand left him, and he heard the echo of her voice saying, "Thank you." And with that, she was gone for good.

EPILOGUE

"Hey guys, I just uploaded another video last night—and look! It already has over three thousand views!" Tom exclaimed as he sat down at the lunch table with his tray. Tom had taken his new experience with the supernatural and magic and turned it into a weekly video channel that had practically become an overnight success. Making the videos seemed to be a really great outlet for Tom. Also, now that he focused on putting all of his conspiracy theories and crazy energy into making the videos, he had become much less annoying to the rest of the group. Sometimes Josh and Clio would even join in as guests on the show, and they would all have a great time with it.

"That's awesome! See, I told you they would like your 'Tom's Top 10' idea!" Clio replied, looking up from Josh's homework paper. "You might want to try it this way," she said to Josh as she scribbled down a new math formula. Josh had no problems asking her for help anymore, as she had really toned down her bossy attitude.

"Thanks, Clio," Josh responded. He would have never figured out that math on his own. "Are we still on for meeting up at Mr. Waters' house after school?" he asked them. After everything that had happened, Mr. Waters had reluctantly agreed to give them magic lessons every Friday, and Josh always looked forward to it.

"You bet!" Clio replied.

"You think he'll actually let us try doing a spell on our own this time?" Tom asked.

"I doubt we'll be able to yet," Clio said.

"I don't know," Josh said, "Last time he said we were pretty close to being ready. Maybe this will be it."

The trio couldn't wait to find out.

That afternoon, they got off the bus and headed to Mr. Waters' house, where they were greeted and led inside. Mr. Waters still looked pretty banged up from his fight with his wife, but he had been getting stronger every day. She had really beaten him magically and physically while they were fighting outside the closet. But Josh thought that the hardest part for Mr. Waters was having to have his wife locked up in a mental hospital. He said it was the only way he knew to make sure she didn't hurt anyone else.

They always had classes and discussions upstairs in the temple room with the pillars, altars, and other oddities all around. There were lots of items wrapped in white cloth, and books that Mr. Waters said were not to be opened. Josh had always been bad for letting his curiosity get the best of him, but he knew that knowing what was under the cloth and in the books would have to wait until he was ready for them. The time for everything to be revealed would come soon enough, and Josh knew that he just had to be patient, no matter how tempting it was to peek.

"I thought it would be fun if we learned about the different kinds of spirits today," Mr. Waters began once everyone had gotten settled. They learned all about the different kinds, from angels and demons to the elementals.

"What about nymphs? What category do they fall into?" Clio asked.

"Ah, yes," Mr. Waters replied, "they're a type of water elemental." An entire discussion opened up from that point, as the trio was curious to know more about the creature that had killed Beatrice. They hadn't talked about what had happened in quite some time, but she still lingered in everyone's minds, especially Josh's.

"So is she really gone for good, now?" Josh asked when the topic of Beatrice had come up.

"Yes, she has finally and completely moved on into the afterlife. Even if we were to try to bring her back again just for a short time, she is so far gone now that it would practically be impossible. She would have to have a good reason to want to come back, but we know that she's made peace with this world, so there's no reason for her to come back," Mr. Waters explained. Josh was a little discouraged, knowing that there was not even a possibility that he would ever see Beatrice again.

That night, Josh had a hard time sleeping. The full moon was shining through his window and keeping him awake. *I wonder what it's like for her on the other side.* He thought. *I hope we made the right decision freeing her spirit.* He got up to close the blinds, and couldn't help but stop as he saw Beatrice's room across the yard.

Goodnight, Beatrice, he thought to himself.

He climbed back into bed. *I hope we can see each other again one day.* He thought as he felt sleep starting to take him.

"We will," he heard a small voice giggle, "Goodnight, Josh."

Check out a preview of the next book in the

FRIGHTVISION

series:

#GraveyardChallenge

(Featuring the nightmares of S. O. Thomas)

CHAPTER ONE

We took turns peeking through the peephole of my front door, like my doorstep had somehow become the scene of a crime. Maybe it had. Harley Jones stood on the other side with a backpack and sleeping bag. Social suicide *was* considered a crime when you were in the seventh grade at Kingsland Prep. I'd spent the better half of last year trying to prove to my new friends that I was worthy of their attention and here she was ripping my efforts to shreds in seconds. My slumber party was for friends only—normal friends who didn't live in graveyards.

Harley's grandmother attempted to reverse her car into the empty parking spot in front of my house for the third time, nearly knocking the bumper off the car in front of it.

I twirled the end of my braid around my index finger, a habit I'd picked up after Mom died in the fire at her dress shop last year, and tried to think of a reason Harley and her grandmother would be here. One that made sense.

"Do you think she's lost?" I glanced at Mina and hoped she didn't think I had anything to do with this.

"Don't ask me." Mina pushed her purple frames back in place and tucked her annoyingly straight black hair behind her ears. She clicked on her phone and swiped through her messages. "Maybe she kidnapped Taryn, stole her invitation, and has her tied up in a basement somewhere. I haven't heard from her since yesterday."

"Neither have I ..." I turned and walked toward the living room where my dad had set up the food. "Maybe she'll go away if we don't answer."

"You'll do no such thing, Q-bear." My father blocked my path to the living room.

Mina giggled.

"Dad ..." My cheeks burned. This party wasn't going at all how I'd planned.

"Sorry ... *Qenna*. I bumped into Harley's grandmother at the supermarket today and she's looking for someone to remodel the funeral home. I told her to bring Harley by tonight so she can hang with you guys while we talk shop."

"Why would you do a thing like that, Mr. Scott?" Mina propped her elbow on my shoulder. I stepped away until her arm fell back at her side.

"Because adults have to worry about paying for pizza and soda so you kids can enjoy your slumber shenanigans."

"But why does she have to be here for you to talk to her grandmother? Can't you do that while we're at school or something? You knew tonight was special. I wanted to spend it with my friends."

"I thought you two were friends."

"Yeah, like forever ago." My voice trailed off. I'd never told my parents that she'd been the weird kid that followed me around like a shadow. Eventually, I started talking to her since everyone thought we were friends anyway.

"I know time moves slower when you're this close to being a teenager," Dad said, "but you weren't ten that long ago."

I looked at my feet. When kids at school had decided anything close to Haunter Harley was strange by association, I tried to find new, less creepy friends. "Whatever." I swallowed my conscience. "She has a sleeping bag. You told her about the party, didn't you?" I folded my arms and tried to give him my sad, pouty face, hoping I could guilt him into telling Harley the sleepover was cancelled, or that I no longer lived here.

"Normally I can't say no to that face, but this time I have to." Dad leaned in and whispered into my ear, "I really need this job, Q-bear. Do me a solid and just let her stay, okay? You'll have fun if you give her a chance."

I hated to admit it, but I could tell this was important to him. He'd been happy lately, happier than I'd seen him since the fire. Plus, he was trying so hard to be a cool dad, I didn't want to add to his many reasons to be sad.

Do me a solid … Who says that? I chuckled and hugged him. "Fine …" I took a deep breath and prepared myself for hurricane Mina. She narrowed her eyes and shook her head.

Dad walked over to the door as I pulled Mina up the stairs toward my room. The *Cats Are People Too* plaque hanging on our front door jingled when Dad opened it. There was no turning back now.

"I'm confused." Mina plopped on my bed and held her chin in her hands. She was giving me the look she usually reserved for sixth graders. I sighed. In making Dad happy, I'd managed to ruin my special night. We should be eating pizza and watching movies by now. Mina looked like she wanted to go home.

"So, you're okay with Haunter-Harley crashing? Do *I* have to be okay with it? Because I'm not." Mina walked over to my window and peeked outside.

"I'm sorry." I thought about trying to explain that it had been difficult for my dad this last year, trying to do everything on his own. It was hard for me too, pretending to care about all the things my friends did, when mostly I just wanted to crawl under the covers and cry. She didn't get it. Yeah she was adopted, but both of her adopted parents were still alive. "Let's get through tonight and we can go back to ignoring her tomorrow."

Mina giggled. She wasn't looking at me anymore, she was looking …

I turned around and found Harley standing behind me and Taryn behind her. Fashionably late was definitely Taryn's style. At least it meant she wasn't locked in Harley's basement. I tried to force a smile. "Um … hey. I didn't hear you come up." I bit on my braid again. Had she heard what I said?

I shot Taryn a pleading look, begging her to save me.

"Hey Haun—um, Harley. My little brother has the same sleeping bag …. Cute." Taryn pushed past, taking a seat next to Mina.

"If you don't want me here, all you have to do is say so and I'll leave when my grandmother is done talking with your dad." Harley directed her statement to me. Her blue eyes bore into mine like she was searching for my soul. I shivered.

"So, you live in the graveyard, right?" Mina walked over to Harley and took her sleeping bag and backpack. She placed them in the corner with the others and pulled Harley over to my bed. "What kind of slumber party will this be if we all just stand around? Sit. Harley, tell us what it's like living with the dead."

"Mina, come on." I tried to communicate with her the way I had with Taryn, but she grinned at me, flipped her hair over her shoulder and looked back to Harley, who hesitated before sitting down.

Mina crossed her arms. "Harley can stay if she's cool with sharing. I've always wanted to know. Do you sleep in a coffin?"

"Mina!" I closed the door, not wanting Dad to hear whatever was about to happen next. "Maybe you should go, Harley. Sorry."

"I'm cool with sharing." Harley smiled. "You'd be surprised how many people ask me that. And yes, I do sleep in a coffin. They're quite comfy."

Taryn's jaw dropped.

"Seriously? I was kidding." Mina inched away.

Harley paused, then covered her face with her hands.

I leaned over. "You okay?"

She peeked up at me and then cackled. "You actually fell for that?" She flopped over onto my bed and held her stomach as she laughed louder.

"It's not that funny," Mina snapped.

"Probably because you didn't see the look on your faces." Harley erupted in a new round of laughter. "Of course I don't sleep in a coffin. I'm not dead. Would you be scared of me if it hadn't been a joke? You have something against coffins? Dead people?"

"Well, no, I—" Mina started.

"Prove it." Harley's face turned serious. "I dare you."

"This is silly." Taryn glanced at me. "Not everyone is comfortable with death."

"The Graveyard Challenge?" Mina asked.

Harley nodded.

I groaned. Anyone in school with access to the internet—a.k.a everyone, including the teachers—had heard of The Graveyard Challenge. You go into the graveyard and take a selfie with a gravestone. It was especially popular at our school since we had a graveyard practically in the center of town. It was just as stupid as every other viral social media challenge. And doing stupid things to avoid sharing our deepest, darkest secrets hadn't been part of my plans.

But Mina didn't take her eyes off Harley. "Dare accepted."

I sighed. "Taryn's right. Tonight was supposed to be fun—movies and pizza. Remember the last time we played Truth or Dare? *Someone* cried." I tried not to look at Mina, but her eyes were like magnets—and daggers. "And that kid fell out of a tree and broke both of his legs. No. That's not how tonight is going to end."

"Maybe *Q-bear* is the one that's scared," Mina said.

I clenched my fists. Dad had promised he'd never call me that in front of anyone outside of these walls. I should have specified that meant him and me only, even if others happened to be here. "Whatever. Accept the dare or challenge or whatever it is. Leave me out of it."

Harley clasped her hands together. "After lights out, we can sneak up to the graveyard. I'm not a monster, you don't have to go alone like the challenge instructs, but you do have to spend at least fifteen minutes in there. Any less and it doesn't count."

Taryn raised an eyebrow. "That's not how Truth or Dare works. Or, the challenge. And how did we get dragged into this?" She shot me a supportive look.

"I never said I wanted to play Truth or Dare," Harley said. "I just dared her to prove she wasn't scared by accepting The Graveyard Challenge on my terms. Then you both joined in and now we're all going I guess. It's all the same to me. I live there, so I don't really have to prove anything. Do I?"

Mina stood. "Sounds like fun. More fun than the lame night *someone* had planned."

My shoulders drooped. I should never have brought up her crying. If I stood in the way now, Mina would never let me forget it. "If we're doing this, someone has to stay behind to take care of damage control in case my dad wakes up and comes looking for us. I'll stay. I'll wait downstairs and tell him I'm getting snacks for everyone else. I'll stay safely up here … waiting … and not running off to camp out in the grave—"

"No," Mina interrupted. "Harley stays. She can be the lookout and we'll go. We'll find something else for her to do."

"How will she know you've actually done it?" Taryn asked.

"The challenge says we have to take a selfie with a gravestone," Mina said. "Can't take a selfie with a gravestone without going into the graveyard. We'll each take one as proof."

"Perfect! But you have to take it with one of the graves next to the dead oak tree. You know, the big one without any leaves. It's far enough from the entrance. If you take the picture there, I'll know you were in long enough. I'll know you didn't cheat."

Mina shrugged. "Can't be that bad. Taryn, you in?"

Taryn looked at me. "You sure you want to do this? Go back there? I know you haven't been there since … well, since the funeral."

Mina plopped back on the bed. "Everything is always about tiptoeing around Qenna and what happened. People die. Life goes on. She's not the only person who lost someone. I never met my parents and you don't see me crying over it. We can leave the baby at home and go without her."

I flinched. I always knew Mina had a mean streak, but she never aimed it with full force at her friends. She wasn't treating me like a friend anymore, all because I embarrassed her in front of a group of people by bringing up the last time she cried. Even though I never said her name, I should have known it was still a sore subject. I couldn't lose anyone else, so I took a deep breath and whispered, "I'm in."

CPSIA information can be obtained
at www.ICGtesting.com
Printed in the USA
BVHW090834010422
632949BV00001B/67